Dinosaur Thunder

Marion Dane Bauer

Margaret Chodos-Irvine

Scholastic Press New York

LIBRARY OF CONGRESS CATALOGING-IN-PUBLICATION DATA
Bauer, Marion Dane.
Dinosaur thunder / by Marion Dane Bauer ;
    illustrated by Margaret Chodos-Irvine. — 1st ed.   p.   cm.
    Summary: Brannon is afraid of thunder until his older brother compares thunder
        to one of Brannon's favorite subjects—dinosaurs.
ISBN 978-0-590-45296-0 (hardcover : alk. paper)
    [1. Thunderstorms—Fiction. 2. Fear—Fiction. 3. Dinosaurs—Fiction.]
        I. Chodos-Irvine, Margaret, ill. II. Title. PZ7.B3262Di 2012 [E]—dc23 2011017099
10 9 8 7 6 5 4 3 2 1   12 13 14 15 16

Printed in China   38
First edition, May 2012

The text was set in Folio Medium and Folio Bold.
The display type was set in P22 Prehistoric Pen.
Illustrations for this book were created using a variety of printmaking techniques and
nontraditional materials, including textured wallpaper, vinyl fabric,
plastic lace, and pencil erasers.
Art direction and book design by Marijka Kostiw

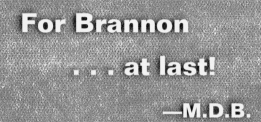

For Brannon

. . . at last!

—M.D.B.

To Bradley,
my thescelosaurus!

—M.C.I.

When lightning flares

in the faraway sky

and clouds growl like lions waking . . .

. . . big brother Chad dances a dance

right in the middle of the room.

"A storm is coming.

A storm is coming!"

Chad shouts.

Brannon looks for   a place to hide.

"Don't be scared,"

Daddy says to Brannon, beneath the bed.

"That thunder is only a big cat purring."

Brannon runs to the window. He knows about cats.

The neighbor's cat scratched him once when

he was only trying to hug her.

Thunder must be a big, big cat.

The

thunder

RUMBLES

louder.

Brannon hides again.

"Don't be scared,"

Grandma says to Brannon, behind the couch.

"It's only the angels bowling in heaven."

Brannon runs to the window. He knows about bowling.

He's gone to the bowling alley with his mom.

He's heard the balls boom along the hard floor.

And he's seen the tenpins tumble.

Maybe they will fall through the clouds!

The thunder

CLATTERS

and BANGS.

Brannon hides again.

"Don't be scared," Grandpa says

to Brannon, inside the closet.

"It's only the clouds bumping together."

Brannon knows about clouds.
They get so big, they can rain
for days and days. They're so dark,
they can wipe out the sun.
What if a cloud bumped into
him? Would he make a
noise like thunder, too?

The thunder says,

"Rum - bum -

BOOOOO

bum-bum

OOOOM!"

Brannon hides again. . . .

"Don't be scared,"

Chad whispers to Brannon, inside the toy box.

"That thunder is only dinosaurs stomping around.

And you know about dinosaurs."

"Dinosaurs?"

Chad is right. Brannon knows about dinosaurs!

Some are **bigger** than cars,
bigger than trucks, **bigger** than houses.
They have **enormous** tails and **colossal** teeth
and **huge** horns, and some have spikes, too.

Brannon knows *all* about dinosaurs.

He knows about **spinosaurus** and **stegosaurus** and **triceratops,** too.

He knows about **allosaurus** and **diplodocus** and **iguanodon.**

Hasn't he always wished

he could have a

Tyrannosaurus rex

for his very own?

"I LOVE dinosaurs,"

Brannon says.

And he comes

ROARING out

to **BOOM**

and **BELLOW.**

He **CLOMPS.**

And he **STOMPS.**

And he **RAGES** and

RUMBLES

with the dinosaur thunder.

Until . . .

"Don't be scared, boys,"

Mama says. "It's only thunder."

Brannon smiles at Chad.

"Don't be scared,"

he tells his big brother.

"It's only
DINOSAUR
THUNDER."

And they BOTH do the

dinosaur
thunder
dance

right

in the middle

of the room!